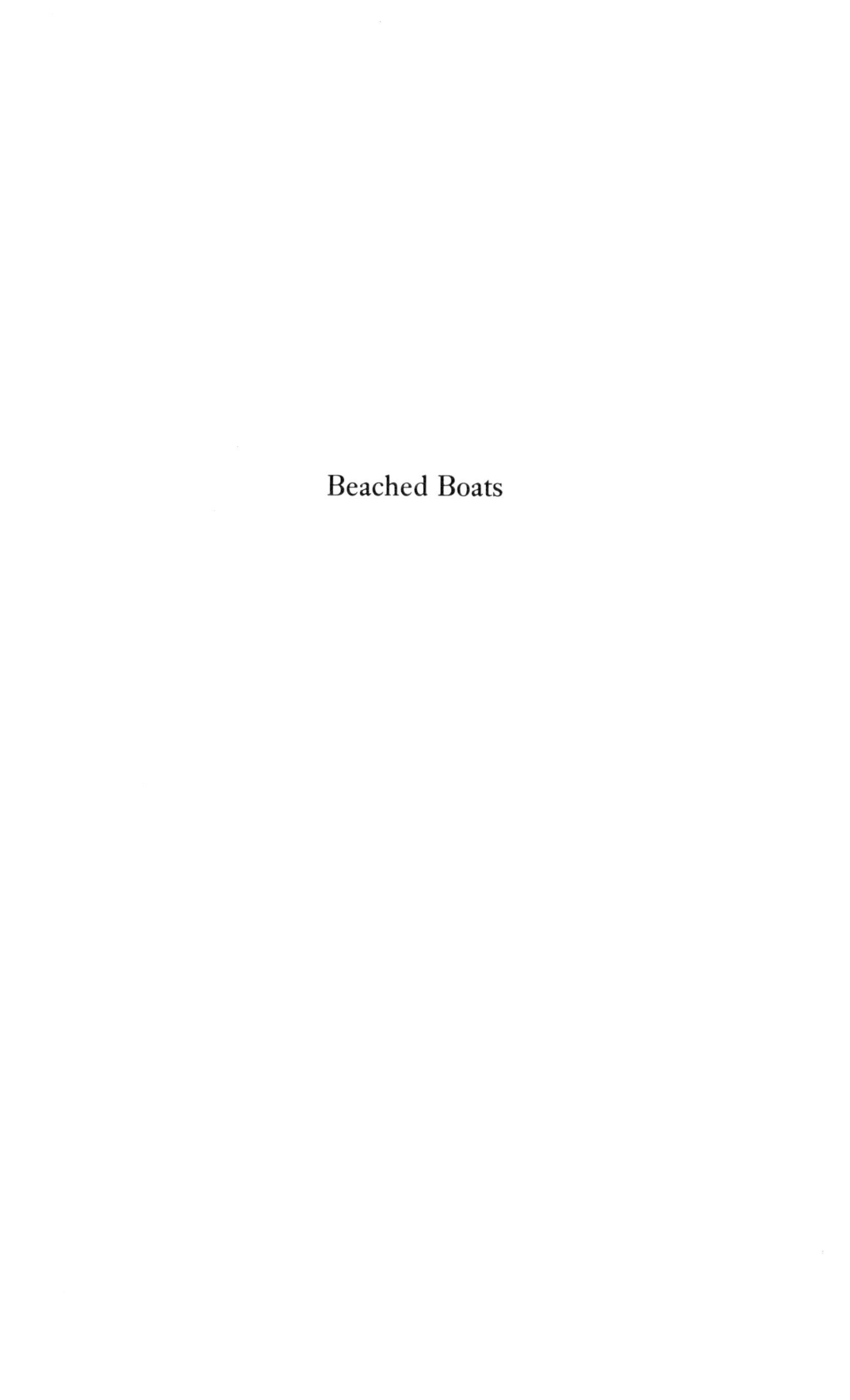

Beached Boats

JENNY JOSEPH
and
ROBERT MITCHELL

Beached Boats

LONDON
ENITHARMON PRESS
1991

First published in 1991
by the Enitharmon Press
BCM Enitharmon
London WC1N 3XX

Distributed in the USA
by Dufour Editions Inc.
PO Box 449, Chester Springs
Pennsylvania 19425

Text © Jenny Joseph 1991
Photographs © Robert Mitchell 1991

ISBN 1 870612 61 2 (paper)
ISBN 1 870612 66 3 (portfolio of signed prints)

Set in 10pt Ehrhardt by Bryan Williamson, Darwen
and printed by
Antony Rowe Limited, Chippenham, Wiltshire

Contents

Beached Boats   10

Beached Boats

A Candle Flame deprived of Air   14

A Candle Flame deprived of Air

Cup of Milk   18

Cup of Milk

Saturday Treat   21
Ant Nest   23
Two Polished Chestnuts   24
Extended Simile   26
Solstices   28
Piece of Wood   29
Jewelled was the Valley   29

Chair   32

Chair

In a Glass   36

A Gift of Flowers   40

A Gift of Flowers

Castles in the Sand   43
Photograph   45
Shawls   46
House in a Wood   47

Diver   50

Diver

Time Waiting   54

Time Waiting

Cormorant   58

Cormorant

and in this presence how much "elsewhere" lurks

Beached Boats

The upturned boat doesn't move. The old boat's gunwhale is jammed hard in the frozen gravel. The children playing in the snow cannot budge it half an inch. Its keel's sharp outline holds an immobile arc in the glimmer of Winter afternoon, a glimmer whose source seems to be the dusk of the shore rather than any last light in the sky;

as the held string of a bow or a stretched hawser cleaves the blank of air with its tension

so the line of the hulls of these beached boats contain the swell of the tides

so, staring cloudlocked on the frozen shore we feel in our muscles their bounding through the water.

A Candle Flame Deprived of Air

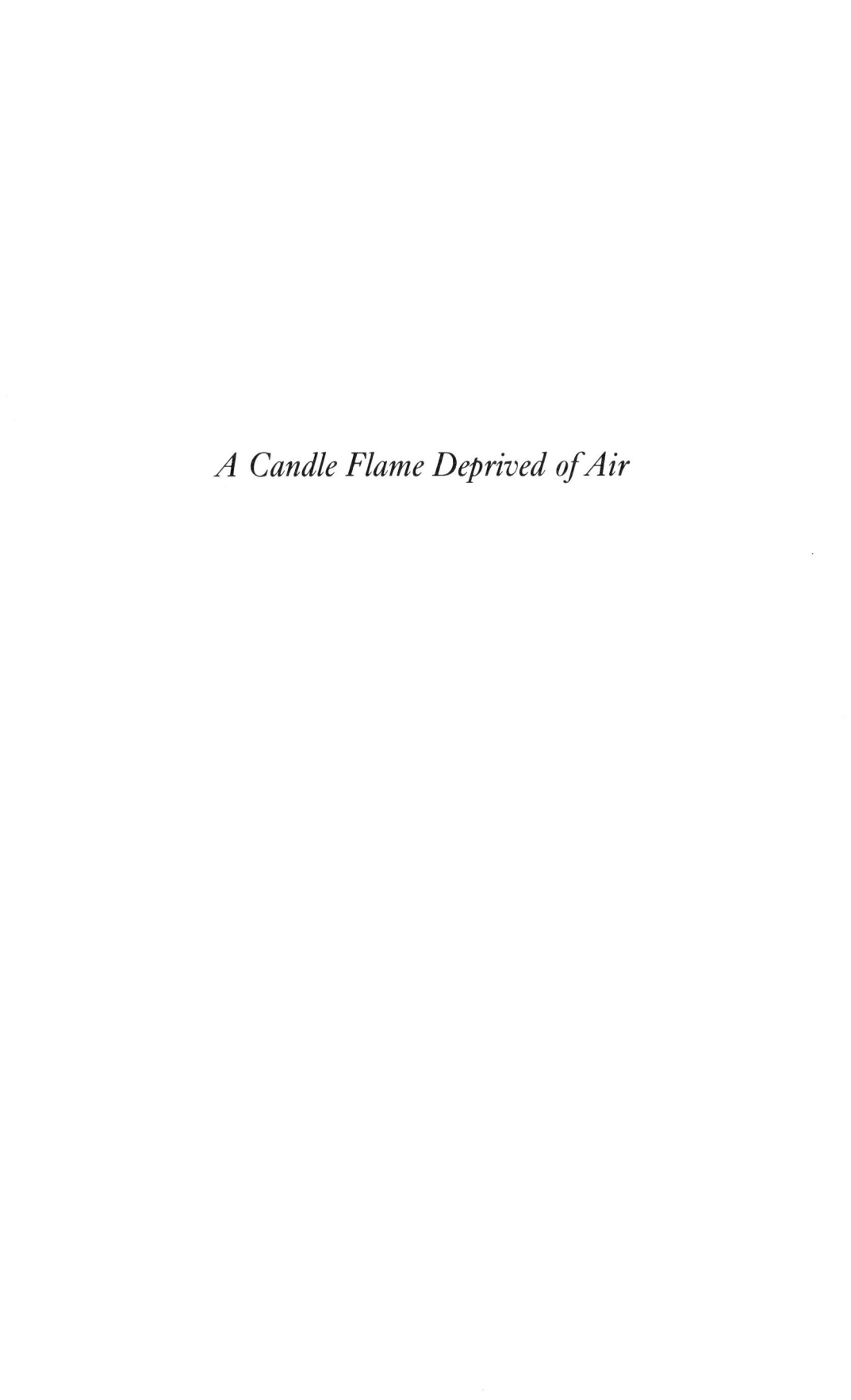

The blue swelling on the tip of the wick quickly climbed into a wavering yellow flame, elongating and pulsating. After a rapid shrinking it rose back a little and settled to a steady cone of light, the yellow surround and the smoky arch within it now of constant proportion. The wall was bathed in a soft clear yellow without shadow.

You put a glass over it to show the child that the candle needs air.

The flame remains but instantly loses its light. It darkens, it sickens, diminishes. It shrinks into itself. It is gone.

The man said very little latterly on his errands to get bread, to pay bills. Then he ceased to go out, though occasionally seen, standing in his open back door, once or twice getting in washing. Then no doors or windows were opened, the curtains hardly ever drawn back. When he first restricted his habitation to his room at the top of the house he yet sat at the table, lit the gas fire, made tea, got up and went to bed. The period was short when he remained in his bed and yet used it like a boat's cabin: reading lamp, tray for food, different positions, sitting up in the day, lying down for sleep. Soon he had pushed it all away and lay, the progress of the day not reaching his shadowed recess, tossing and turning sometimes though moving as if in an attempt to shift a burden from his chest, to get air. Once turned on his side facing the wall he did not turn back. He lay quite still. Gradually his knees started to move up and his shoulders shrank down as if a caterpillar should very slowly turn in on itself. When his right elbow was on his knee and his head pushed into the crook of his arm beneath the stale blankets in the airless dark there was no further movement he could make.

Cup of Milk

A trickle which if spilt would only make a puddle on the table, opaque wetness held between the ribs of the worn wood on this old table – lees which if rinsed out in the sink would make only thinly milky, grey-white, a pint of water, if you yet pour it into this small cup makes a globe of milk.

This chunky solid bulbous coffee-cup you can hold in the curled palm of your hand as an egg in an egg-cup. The drop of milk fills this small cup just rightly to the brim as the cup fills your hand, nourishment not waste, full white infill, cup used for holding, not space prone to shadow and bits falling in but cup of fullness, cup of achievement, same quantity vehicle and content.

Hold the cup steady in your hand, each hour as it falls softly through the day easy with activities: chopping wood on a fine day, cleaning a bit, the letter written, information garnered, the errands to pay bills, deliver things; food prepared, stores laid in, the drop saved against another round to-morrow, actions laid up against the dark. Hold the cup steady,

and at the right time if the swing of the axe is right in conjunction with its angle the wood splits into soldiers almost of itself. You do not need to flail if you let it drop right – poise and let drop, as the hours fall with a quiet but firm settling (moving in rhythm as drifting leaves find definitely their proper place if the swaying is not disturbed by intrusion of thwart winds);

at that moment which is recognized rather than known, rather than decided on, rather than aimed at, without thought, but in an interval of concentration between thought,

as if in libation, but not jettisoned,

lift it to your lips and drink.

Saturday Treat

A piece of fruit cake she would have. She hovered over the tray with gateaux and the tray of fancies.

Well, fruit cake anyway, that was easy. She always had that, and let me see...

Tom came for her every Saturday from work which on that day he finished at 12 and they went to the football. On the way he bought them pie and mash at a place that sold eels. She nearly always had the same, what he had, meat pie. She enjoyed going down the road with everyone streaming towards the ground. There were usually enough people they knew to wave or shout out to. You wouldn't hardly notice it on other days if you didn't know there was a football ground at the end of it.

It would be easier just to buy more of the fruit cake. She knew Tom did like that but with all those other things it was a pity not to try something different.

After the match they came back to her room and had the tea she had got ready earlier.

The other cakes might be more expensive than she thought. She knew the price of the fruit cake.

Saturday mornings were pleasant with the feeling that the rest of the day was taken care of. In the evening they went to the cinema and afterwards for a drink at the Feathers. They liked to be on their way home before the fish shop shut so they could buy chips to eat with the cups of milky coffee she always made when they got in. They would put on records and Tom stayed about an hour and a half. She usually bought a new record when she got her pay on Friday.

The creamy ones looked very inviting but they upset her stomach. The once or twice she'd given in to their surface attraction she had been a bit disappointed. They didn't taste of much and left you still wanting. "Is it real cream?" she asked the girl behind the counter who gazed out of the window with the cake tongues raised waiting for her decision. Whichever the girl said would be her excuse for saying no. "What's in those little pies?" "They're crumble tarts. Apple or cherry. They're nice." "I'll have two of those. Two cherry."

She hadn't bought a new record this week. She'd gone with Lesley in the office to a disco last night. Up West. They'd spent quite a lot getting there and back. She wished Tom liked dancing and would take her Up West.

The tops of the fruit pies were all crusted with sugar with a dark red ooze where they joined the rim which was hard-baked. Something to get your teeth into but juicy and refreshing to the taste. "Oh but I'll still have the fruit cake," she said. "You've got to let yourself go sometimes, haven't you?"

"She'll go back to two lots of fruit cake next week I expect" the girl who had served her said to the other one, who was new and diligently wiping down trays. "She always does. You see. I don't know why she has to take so long choosing the same thing."

She chose two cakes as if for lovers.

Ant Nest

As the establishment of an ant citadel under the top soil makes desert a considerable area which yet shows a green surface, extending the sterility of the soil by the continuance of multifarious activity below, concentrated, un-remitting, aborbing, unseen,

resulting in a lack of hold in such plants as go on attempting to grow on the soil for they have to survive with a very curtailed rooting system, (the honey-combed areas retain no moisture and have no nourishment)

So the death of his child years ago, unknown to most of his acquaintance, a wound covered over with courage, and determination to continue alive in this world, laid beneath layers of activity – the walking tours with his brother, the visits, in Spring and Autumn usually, to his wife's parents on the Welsh borders, the bringing of their skiff in off the river for the Winter, the fruit-picking at the farm in the vale of Evesham for his wife to make jam, the sending off for tickets for when the National Companies came to Worcester,

apparent coverage as bright and solid as a full herbaceous border,

So this grief chawing away made a place riddled with holes beneath all the associations, all his filling of his days. When he cracked up in the office over something that would not have worried a junior his colleagues emphasized their disbelief by repeating how perfectly well he had been and normal and competent, with no sign even in the previous day or two that anything was worrying him,

but anyone who knew about soil conditions and the ravages a colony of termites makes on substance if left undisturbed would have recognized the ashen skin and lethargy of the man as consequential. The unseeing stare, foredone; closure; concluded;

For there was no body to it, no nourishment to be had from it, all used up and made useless by the life of emasculation perpetually at work below the surface, taking all good from it, preventing conditions of soil recovery whatever was manfully done on the surface up in the air by a few tenacious plants.

Two Polished Chestnuts

The chestnuts in the mud of the ditch looked valuable objects, like old polished desk fitments, so you had to pick them up, to save them, to cherish them.

Colour is determined by the eye (a decision in the brain) but this light that shines at you as if speaking to you from the polished flank seems reflected from deep within. The rich polish is deep laid in the solid piece in your palm, as the gleam of good hair comes from health at source. And then they lie dull on the mantelpiece. Dusty then wrinkled. Getting nasty. The fish whose gleam, whose flash whose quick flick of colour along its back (its taut belly paler) led us on, ever escaping, ever alive, cool and lustreful, lies flaccid on the grit stone of the quay. Unappetizing, eye glazed, dimming, stinking.

Some years later (life-times if you computed by the different circumstances each had worked their way through in the interval) they were at the same time in the same place – a fête in aid of the local hospital. He still sported, if not the style that had been for the young when she had met him, yet a style for the young of some fashion passed. He had not been young then, when they had met, though she had been. She must then, she thought, have seemed like one of this current batch of faithful-dog hangers-on wanting to be the one most useful to his major-domo-ing of the occasion. It hadn't been Friends of the Hospital then but something on the fringes of the political, organizing a placard-carrying event in the campaign to unionize the catering trade at the restaurant where she had been working. She must have lost three jobs in the feverish two months she'd had to do with him. How forgotten that time!

It was easy for her to avoid him. He was very taken up with the setting-up of a first-aid demonstration in the marquee. How could I ever have touched him, she thought, glancing to confirm that it really was him but anxious lest her look should alert his. She had not been particularly satisfied with life earlier that day and was now extremely glad to be her, she who had been his acolyte, who had wanted so much to be a part of anything, everything he did that she would have swapped skins. Incredible! She put an extra pound in the collecting box at the gate as she went out in expiation of the disloyalty she felt, not to him, for she had done more than keep her word long after she knew him to be chaff, but to her own past self, and in gratitude for her own life far away from all that now.

The owner of the holiday house was having a clear-out getting the house ready for the next let. Those mouldy lumps on the mantelpiece, old conkers were they, picked up on some walk? People didn't seem able to go a walk without bringing things back from the woods, or if they visited the village, fish from the quay for her to cook or plants to be looked after. She swept them off with other accumulated rubbish on to the fire she'd lit to clear the grate. They flamed with a dim blue lick of fire and glowed dully into crumbles of ash like two fragments of coal, giving off a small warmth.

Extended Simile

As when   in a tree, the centre having been struck with some disease the crest flourishes among the crowns of the forest, nourished through its surface and kept straight in storms even, by the surrounding growth, yet seeming green and sappy will one calm day crash its length in ruin making a trenched gash on the clad hill-side;

as when   a rock face, solid slab from eternity, weathered, weathering, formed mainly of one substance but with a rift of softer material, lime in granite say, concealed in its core, splits and crumbles away, tumbling through the air that has teased out its fault;

as when   tree root bursts up flaking the splitting rock it grew from, each other's downfall, to shrivel in the light, to pulverize to loose shards,

so   "Why didn't you ask me what sort I wanted?" she says. "You knew I'd be in soon but of course you can't wait a minute once you feel like doing something, though it doesn't matter how long we hang about for you." "I thought I could save a job and get it for you." "You ought to know by now it's just going to give me extra to do because it'll be me that goes and changes it. I could've got it myself in the first place with less bother";

so   "I'll not hurry home," he thought, "I can pretend I forgot it was her evening at the clinic. The times I've hurried and nothing's been ready. Only let myself in for some work. If I get in at the last moment she'll have seen to the children and she'll just have to shoot out and there won't be time for talk";

so   she scrapped and scraped and snapped the new man who would have been kind;

so   he crumbled and slid down, no hold for what would have grown again, sheltered in surety;

so   an avalanche down the dry cliffside, no foothold in scree of shale, the gash of their ruin seen far across the valley

         harmed by an old hurt
         leaning on a central flaw

cause;
agent;
effect.

Solstices

Swing up round into the dark nook by the wall, out of hot baked glare on the road into dark under the copper beech on the corner, then on into light again, the car going on up until the next swing round into the open, the heat-hazed valley all laid open below, and round and up again, gears changing beautifully, round and along and up again into the high hot clear air, making for home, known pleasures, lovely, lovely day

nothing more to do, absolute. Heat, midday, full, Summer.

And could death be like this – apogee – a finishing, a perfection, a finale and held note on the major of cold iced sun, for death is cold but in no other way may need to be different; burst of a completed sun, burst and unwavering beam of the dark dazzle off the freeze, as this off the white light of Summer? Absolute, nothing more to do, laid open.

Why not?

Happy in the Summer, joyful greeting in shaded streets of even strangers on their way to things; the explosion of the poppy as it shoots its bolt, balanced pole, quivering needle stayed at the upright before it slides down again

On the same axis lies the other Pole, the ending, the release, the last tender touching of the fading face, communion of even strangers over the finishing, the clutch relaxed, nothing left to do, laid down; for the line that goes through it is the one line through all three points, fulcrum and Poles. Swing down, ease down, away from the needles exploding from the cold, into the shade, then further down through cold again, down, away – the same point of attainment, of halt, of rest reached after all the oscillation in between.

Piece of Wood

You catch sight of a piece of wood between waves as the light catches the curve of water it settles down over; it lifts with the heave of the water moving on, then slides back into its trough again where it settles to its own purposes. Balancing and swinging, accommodating to the wrappings of water, it nudges, sways down through the layers going its own thwart direction, sideways balancing till it is far away across the limitless coruscations of the sea that are the waves coming on their unchanging frontal path towards

as a key, covered in the folds of cravats, piles of sheets, the dips and folds of cloth, spaces in stuff – balls of wool, lining, bales of rugs, stacks of sloping yielding supporting surfaces, – slips down, works across, now wrapped and trapped with the lifting of the pile, now on the move again, settling, travelling

our intentions slip through our days.

Jewelled was the Valley

Jewelled was the valley, thick with sparkles of light, and then higher up unevenly scattered over, the dark mass of the wooded hill. At the densest dark, up near the imperceptible line where dark bulk became dark space, were one or two far separate points, as if a single pearl had been dropped here and there from a hand clutching a broken necklace, no longer able to keep them all in before releasing them into the basket it was moving over.

Two walkers climbed up out from the sparkled valley over the dark edge which was backed by soft cloud, and up again and out on to the high hidden road.

Chair

Coming down in the night to get some water I do not wish to disturb the breath of the dark by turning on the light. The house was warm and peaceful. I went back to my room as if from sitting in the dark by someone sleeping, sleeping well, breathing regularly with no sound.

It is very quiet in the house, very still. There is no one to see the chair in the hall, but it stands there as the slight thinning of the night before Summer dawn begins its outline, begins to define it out of the block of the dark

as a painter, by brushing in a focus on space, might make emerge bar back, plane of wood, dimension where a person may sit.

So all we can do to recognize the object is to listen to the air at the point where it laps it, listen to the waves of light beating up against bar back, slender frame, wooden seat. As the light breathes stronger, separating the chair from the dusk in the hall, it moves out into definition against the white wall;

the chair is placed, poised, by the light. It holds in its shadowed seat all who have sat there, all those who may come.

In a Glass

We went into the huge building and I was glad we had come; glad too at your pleasure that we had managed to include in your visit one of our monuments.

There were innovations since I last showed someone London's symbol for awe. There was a big revolving door, no doubt to keep the temperature even inside the cathedral so the cold Easter winds should not snatch away the heat and make soar the heating bills; and make shiver the visitors and make miserable those standing in wonder looking up into the dome.

We gazed at the beautiful black and white diamond flagged floor with the small stone inset commemorating plainly those fallen. St Paul's was full of people, as it was intended to be, admiring, exclaiming, going to and fro like a town on market day; looking, sitting thinking. It was a lucky stroke that the grandeur and pleasantness of London was working and that we'd come this way.

But what I remember apart from the glow of your appreciation, what I see when I think of the occasion, what I see it through, is the special new glass of the revolving doors that in fact you can't see through; for as we came up to them they threw back the reflections of the people coming up the steps on to the portico, your eager face, the skirts of a mack swinging open, street furnishings, roof edges of buildings down Ludgate Hill. We faced the sky behind us, the outside world, then our own stretched and funny figures lurching towards the centre; and like a road which swallows a car at the horizon in a film shot, all those coming up to the edifice had their reflections pulled in, twirled round, and disgorged invisibly, for you could not see into the nave, you could not see those who had been landed on the other side, inside; only their reflections surging round as someone else pushed in.

The people were shepherded warm and shadowless within the great shell, their shadows, their reflections, their seeking images shut out and twirled away into the air outside. The irregular muffled thud of the door swinging round separated the unseen real bodies from the clear sharp outlines of what after all has no body, no being; eyes that gaze but cannot see, cannot answer others', breathing skin and lips that do not even mist the glass that holds them and that withdraw behind the brittle block of the surface at the touch of fingers on the glass.

A Gift of Flowers

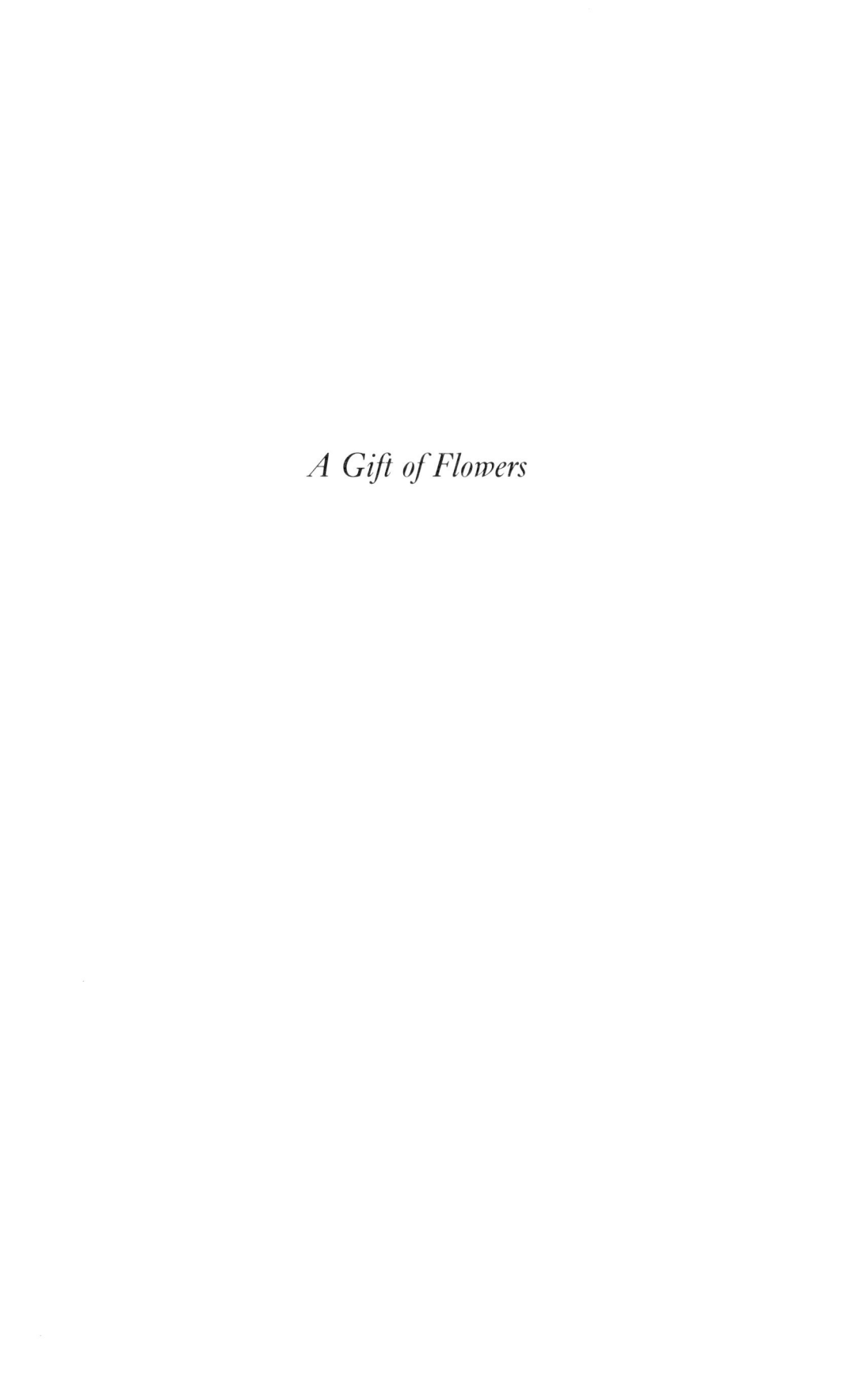

The gift of flowers, the bowl of the tulip like the comfort of a sympathetic child's hand on the taut face, on the wracked head, cup-like little hand, healing;

the gift of flowers, the spray of mignonette like the eyes that fill with tears at your sorrow;

the gift of flowers, a person who crosses the room and says come with me I'm going your way I'll get you home.

And I look now at the stubby point of the iris, the white blobs which are carnation buds, a few tinged with pink opening out, flecked with pink on the back side of the opening frilled petal, and the spray of three buds leaning on the other side against the wall, and the fuzzy blue, in the dusk of that part of the room on the mantel-piece only blue because I know it's blue,

a loving-one's flowers, as if to say "don't give up, don't stop doing kind things, don't give in to the warping world, there are other sorts. The harm these tyrannies do is to make you see the world like that. There are other things. People can spit poison at you, but people can give you comfort. There are healings, there are joys. Here are some flowers."

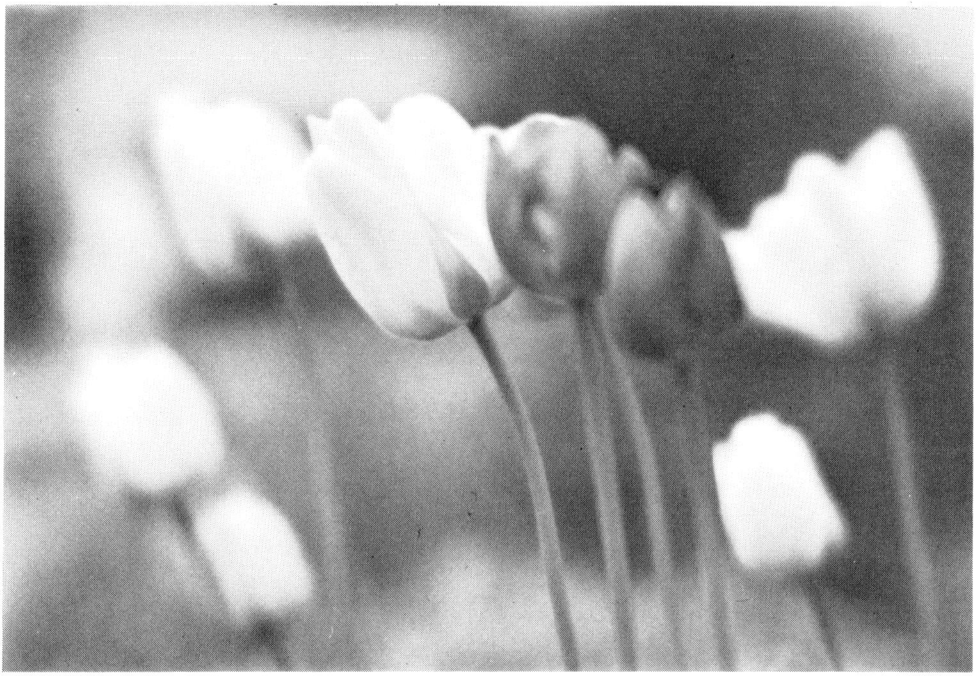

Castles in the Sand

A man scoops the sand up into a pile. The long sea rollers run continuously from the horizon. He scoops it into a pile and carves it as if it were rock. We see the grains and the ease of the little knife he uses so it is still sand though it is becoming a wall, a castle, and carved and shaped as if from rock.

But it is a picture. The camera shows us windows, arches, buttresses, rising quicky formed at once. It perhaps took hours. The walled cities out of rock took years. That is the pleasure of toys. The blanc-mange cat, dolls' house life, the model lighthouse, there is not the tedious and perpetual push of recalcitrant material, the time it takes for the blood to circulate, the years for peat to form. The sands of the Yangtse took centuries to be pressed into rock. Thought, imagination, is in a different time-scheme from getting across the town, wringing out the washing, taking a boat out on the river, processing the picture, placing the page. Getting clothes on and putting a girdle round the earth happen at the same moment in the morning but inhabit utterly separate times. Winged thought indeed.

The building of sand is taking shape, has become the battlements of a city, for the camera moves and we are as if on a cliff. Placing its object the positioning of the shot has placed us, has put us high up in the sea air looking down the cliff-like side of this immense bastion as if into a dark narrow alley far below. How massively they built in those days. You think of the great cliff-sided well-like courts, the bluff sides of tall tenements in Edinburgh down flights of steps, you look up at the patch of sky and are dizzy, hemmed in by cliff-like man-made structures out of the rock of Edinburgh, as if hewn. Medieval castles perched above the abyss rise from the crags of the Rhine gorge as if spurs of rock have grown fairy-tale pinnacles as a tree's branch becomes complicated with leaves.

Then we are further off. It is as if we have been moved back and we then approach it from a distance, the sea in relation, the light on the shore which the waves are running up and the finished structure on the beach as if in a frame. The hands that we saw close up scraping and flicking, the little blade touching up the inside of the miniature arch, are now in proportion to the man who stands beside the castle he has made. We have moved back and what we now see is a man who takes a picture. His hands hold a camera. He takes a picture of the castle and we see the blank paper he pulls out as if we were watching it with him. A picture of the structure on the beach beside the sea materializes on the paper and becomes clearer and behind the edges of the picture of the photo is the sea-shore scene, which is itself a picture.

And as the picture of the photograph makes it look as if it's becoming clearer so the castle that the man has actually built begins to be knocked down by the sea and the wind, or rather, looking at the television screen as if we were looking through a window on to a scene, it seems as if there had been a building that a man had taken a picture of and that the sea and the wind destroyed, as if there were a sea and a wind, as if it was sand as if it was rock as if it was carved into the likeness of a huge complicated rabbit-warren of a building as fancy as Milan cathedral as if it was destructible as sand again. Little grains. It was made of little grains. The focus shifts. The titles move up through the oncoming breakers. They say that the picture, what we see, is made up of black and white grains, you see them when things are out of focus.

The film was called Chateaux de Sable. A castle as if it were of sand. Sand as if it were a castle. A picture as if it were a castle. Chateaux de sable as we should say sandcastles. But what a thing is like is never the same as what it is. Sandcastle and chateau de sable are not quite the same, chateaux de sable is like Chateaux en Espagne or as we say in English: castles in the air – of sand, of air, as if.

Photograph

You can change the details on a photograph. You can do trick photography to put a mini-skirt on a 1930s' sepia bathing belle. In this version different weather blows out over the line of the coast that in that print was a picture in the sun before they built the power station. A figure emerges through the trees, a ghost called up by a smudge on the negative, tampering with time by making a mark on space.

And here on the floor is sat a small solid triangle. No flouncy baby's dress, no woolly rug or black velvet background, brushed hair and ribbon, no chippendale on which stands perfectly central and polished, the polish reflected in the polished table, the rosebowl for calling cards.

The photographer carried his heavy gear back out of the tradesman's entrance long ago, but the floppy raised paw, the sideways glance up, the "when will they find out?" look that he captured half a century ago has come out on this recent snap in the huge batch of prints we've just collected from Boots. A delayed mechanism indeed, an image re-turned, a double exposure.

It is as if one of the old batch had got mislaid and arrived now, the disappearance of the village shop fronts – the haberdashers, the hairdressers with a pale green model of "Eugene" in the window in what was then a side-road, the ironmongers, the photographer's studio next to the coal office on the slope up from the station – notwithstanding. As if "clearing out we came across this old negative. We thought you might like to have it." As if two negatives got superimposed, some detail of the pattern in the cloth so strong that it came through the dye. Delayed process indeed, double exposure with the past showing through the present like a shadow on the lense.

The snap is of a new baby crowded round with adoring people for her first birthday. It is not a "once upon a time" background but our untidy living room, our little lump of love sitting there, sly half-smile and great blue gaze ("What *is* it you've got there? Come on, give it to Mummy") reaching me across fifty years.

Soon she'll get Russian dolls for Christmas; and move up one size in twenty years' time.

Shawls

We walked into the garden as day lifted the sky and here and there on the dark hedges lay white patches, fine wool stuff soaking wet with droplets that made them seem shrunken pieces of fallen mist, like little bits of out-of-place snow still solid when the field round it is warm and green again, finest fairy wool stuff pieces spread to whiten under the dry moon and caught by the danks and darks of night.

Only close up did you see the thousand threads of the fabric, large cobwebs visibly engorged by the wet on them.
It was as if shawls of lightest wool, the softest merino, had been placed here and there delicately with no pressure, no weight on tired bones, as when the gentleness of love puts with a light touch a fine scarf round frail shoulders baby-soft fabric nestling up to gossamer wisps of white hair.

Some gentle love had floated down these drifts, these shawls of dew and they remained there undisturbed on the dark evergreens well into the clear day.

House in a Wood

"...there are some moods like houses, long unvisited..."

We went up the steps to the house. It was long unvisited. We walked up lightly as if we came there frequently, in daily life, like going into the baker's.

But it had been years, another life, since we had even been in the neighbourhood, into the woods; or indeed taken any Sunday afternoon walk, exploring, looking about us, noticing for the next time; it had been another life in which then returning home across the frosting fields with a smoking pink horizon fading like a wisp of fire behind us, we came in to tea at dusk, curtain drawn bright fire. Passed as a dream, that time; and like a dream sometimes suddenly that time jumped fully clothed in all its detail unaccountably in the path of our day.

Groundsel and tufts of grass were growing in the corners of the steps. Lichen and moss on one of the balustrades had flaked patches of the stone. There was no tumbled rubble to push our feet through though. The steps were in surprisingly good condition. The door opened with a light push and we held our breaths for what waft of fungus coming up from skeleton joists, what dead rats, bundles of rotting rags, blackened cans, broken bottles at the edge of circles of ash and half-burnt parts of chairs; what results of neglect and absence.

But we walked into a furnished house. It was uninhabited but not empty, the rooms, like moods, biding their time, available.

We could have come here at any time just like this so easily. Why, we wondered then, had we not done so simple and desirable a thing? It must have been that it seemed we could not.

Friends, keep your establishment. For much of the time I have not been very far tho' often thrown wide by the network of paths and earth-works; misguided by seeming tracks, distracted from your centre, distrained, it must have seemed to me then. One winter afternoon as dark comes down and you settle to the fire and the room and shut out the night and the night's inhabitants, forbear to draw the curtains on the side window that looks across the garden to the wood. The light and the movement of the fire will show me where I am, and easily, naturally – long-unvisited friends – I will walk up the steps and find myself with you.

Diver

Naturally when we meet to talk you ask me how am I, what have I been doing, what seen? as, naturally, that's what I've come to tell you –

Waking we come up through layers of sleep, as divers do who wait to break the surface, breathe the air, fill their lungs with the waking world again –

to breathe the air, and tell you all that was held with the breath, all that was down there, in the depths.

I turn, moving in wide circles, moving slowly, coming to in the air and as I emerge the rope sinks backwards beneath the surface, uncoiling gravitationally into invisibility, in a mirror movement to my rising up to greet you

as in the day one might catch a glance of something, a blue pullover lying at an angle
and think, was that in my dream then, that the child gave it me, or is the recognition of the shape of the elbow of the left arm where it is worn a glimpse from the shifting past, obscured at once by swirling particles of mud that the groping stick stirs up – something buoyant being released through the surface up into the air that makes it visible, to sink at once into the next suck of the current, fathoms down out of reach, out of sight, out of the day,

leaving me with no cable, no support, little choice but to shut the door behind me and go out into the light of day, with not so much as a good story to tell of where I've been, what done, to you who kindly ask how am I?

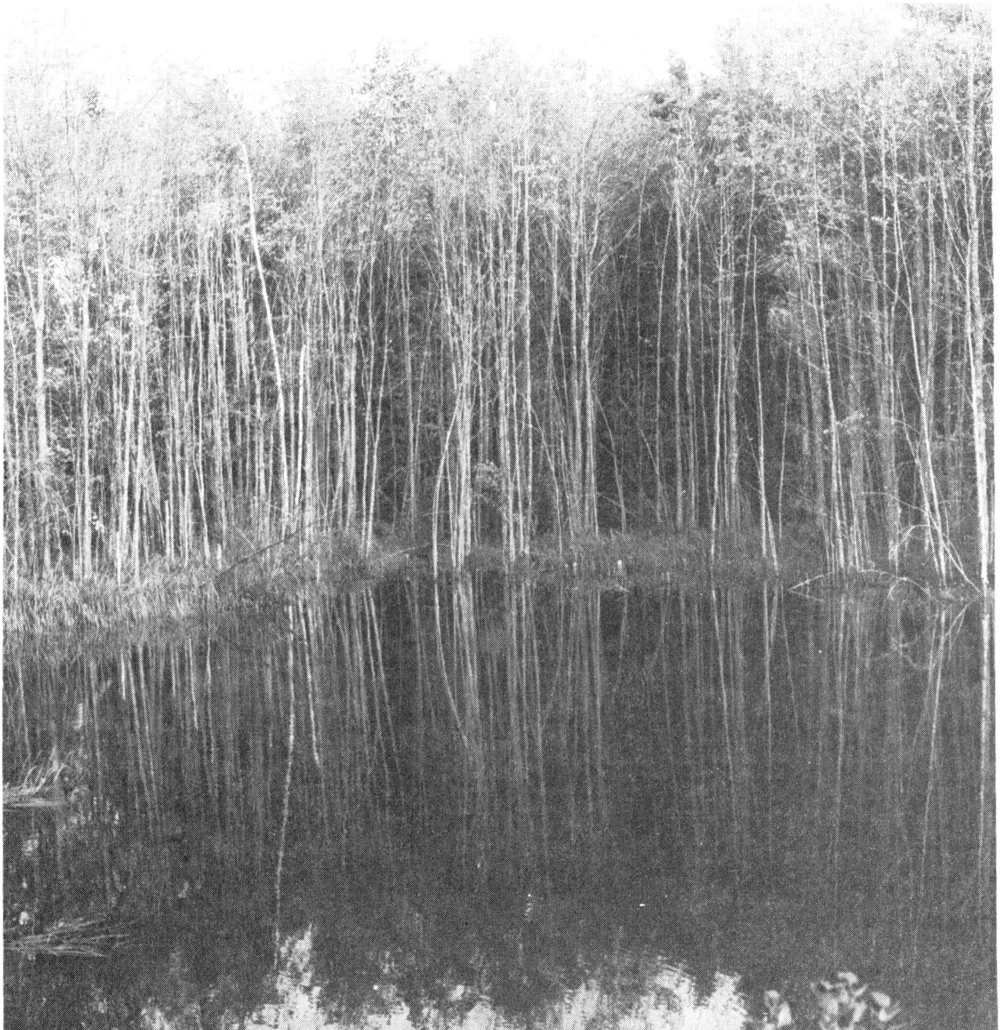

Time Waiting

She came into the house after a bustling Saturday, errands, friends, shopping in the town. She came in full of expectation and was disappointed that there was no letter, no message, nobody waiting for her or possibilities of using this fine Spring evening. The cars slowing down for the junction continued up the hill. The birds, children and dogs subsided.

As the light shifted, withdrawing imperceptibly from the walls and ceiling in the room she sat in, she realized the place was not empty. What the house held – day after day moving through it with its cargo of light and air, with all that had gone on in it: the visits, the good times, the struggles – it had kept for her, as a book holds the life that went into it long ago and seems gone: life left in store for when someone shall come and release it, and make a channel for it again, people the hours while the book is read again.

She *was* looked for. She *was* expected. She had kept the assignation, which she would not for worlds now interrupt even by the click of turning on the light. It was time that was waiting.

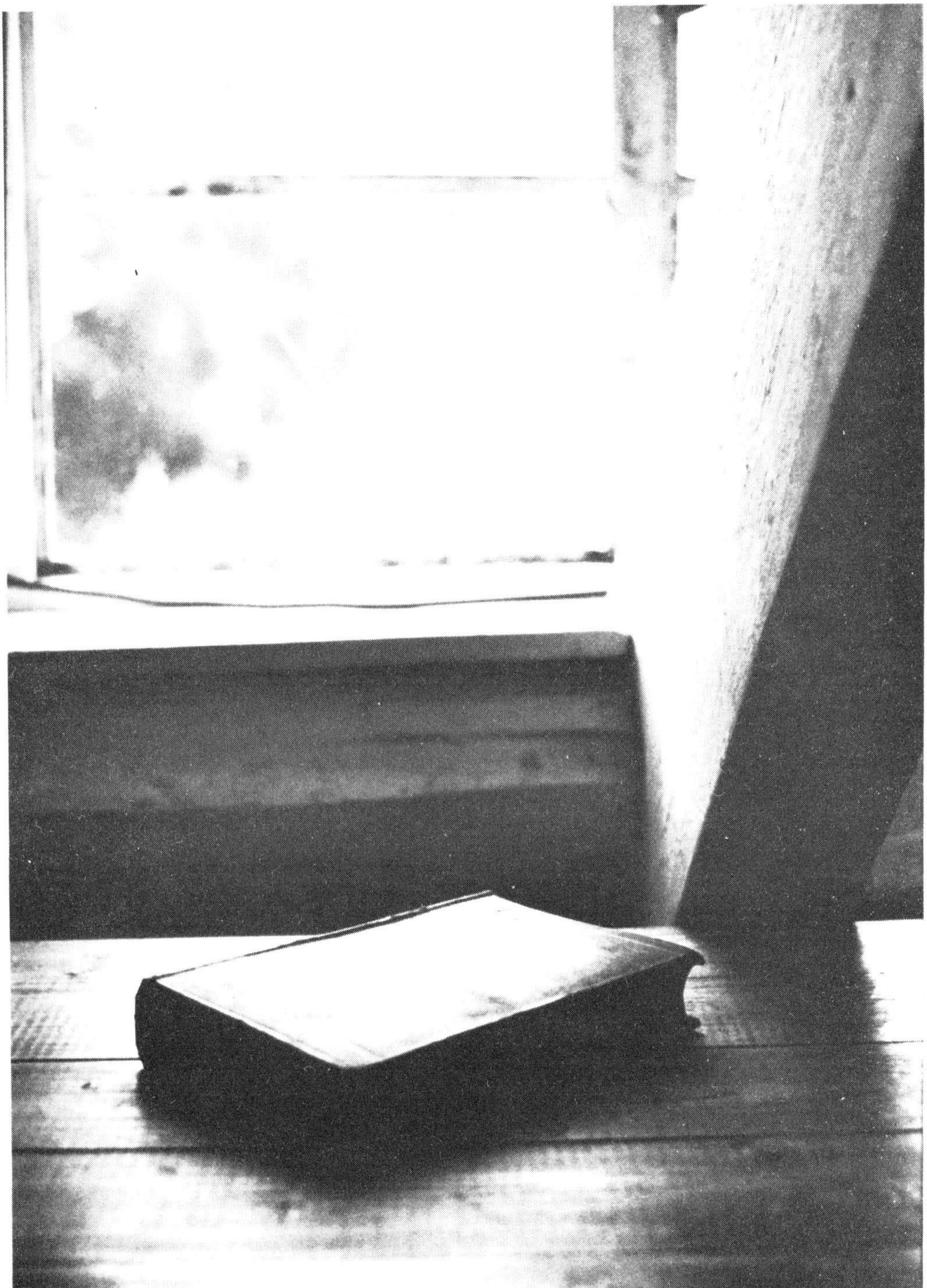

Cormorant

"Private. Keep out." (Notice on foreshore)

Who can own the sea? I can, I can, say the Americas.

The hulk in the bay, and the gulls' cry with the ocean's voice in it, harsh and mournful echo free on the wind

Say otherwise.

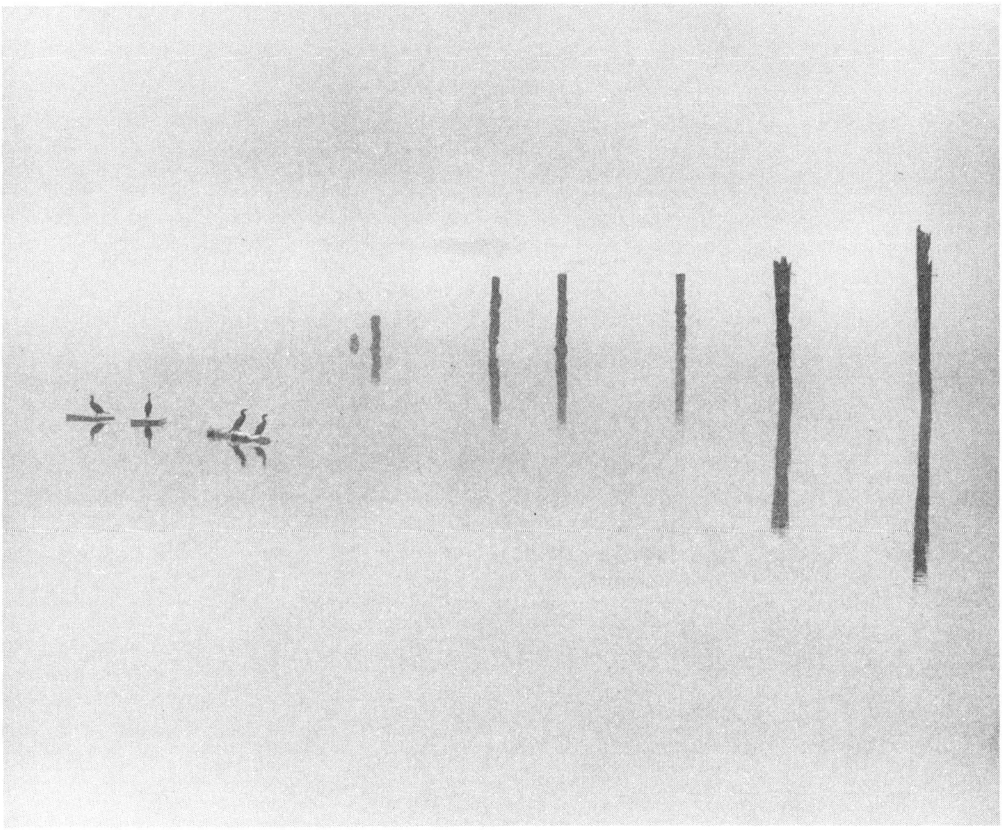